Christmas in Virginia

KAYLA LOWE

Want a free book? Sign up to my newsletter to get my award-winning book for free! www.authorkaylalowe.com

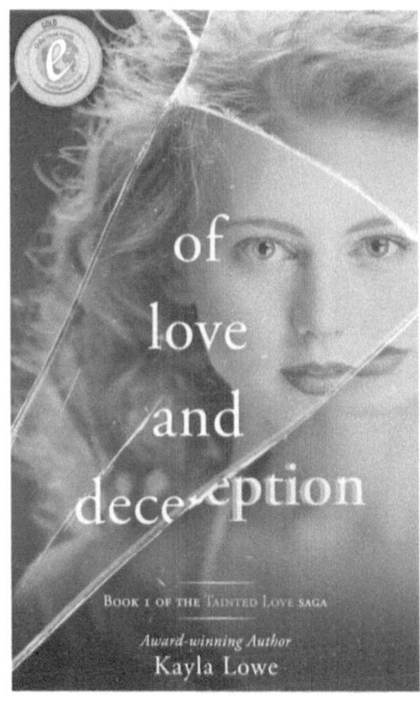

More of My Books

Series

Christmas Blessings

Christmas Miracle for Two
A Christmas Promise of Love
A Christmas of Renewed Faith

Women of the Bible Fiction

Ruth
Esther
Rachel
Hannah
Deborah

Charms of the Chaste Court

A Courtship in Covent Garden
Whispers in Westminster
Romance in Regent's Park
Serenade on Strand Street
Treasure in Tower Bridge

Sweet Honey by the Sea

The Beekeeper's Secret (Book 1)
A Royal Honeycomb (Book 2)
Bees in Blossom (Book 3)
Honeyed Kisses (Book 4)
Blooming Forever (Book 5)

Strawberry Beach Series

Beachside Lessons (Book 1)
Beachside Lessons (Book 2)
Beachside Lessons (Book 3)

Panama City Beach Series

Sun-Kissed Secrets (Book 1)
Sun-Kissed Secrets (Book 2)
Sun-Kissed Secrets (Book 3)

The Tainted Love Saga

Of Love and Deception (Book 1)
Of Love and Family (Book 2)
Of Love and Violence (Book 3)

Of Love and Abuse(Book 4)
Of Love and Crime (Book 5)
Of Love and Addiction (Book 6)
Of Love and Redemption (Book 7)

Standalones

Maiden's Blush

Poetry

Phantom Poetry
Lost and Found

Chapter One

Lauren's car rolled to a stop at the familiar intersection, the old traffic light swaying gently in the crisp December breeze. Her eyes lingered on the faded "Welcome to Oakridge" sign, its peeling paint a testament to the passage of time. A smile tugged at her lips as she breathed in the scent of pine and woodsmoke that wafted through her cracked window.

"Home sweet home," she murmured, her fingers drumming a soft rhythm on the steering wheel.

As the light turned green, Lauren eased her foot off the brake, allowing her car to glide down Main Street. The storefronts, decked out in twinkling lights and garlands, beckoned to her like old friends. She couldn't help but chuckle at the sight of Mr.

Thompson's hardware store, its windows still plastered with the same faded posters she remembered from childhood.

Some things never change, she thought, a warmth spreading through her chest.

Her gaze drifted to the old oak tree in the town square, its bare branches now adorned with hundreds of colorful ornaments. Memories flooded back—of hot cocoa sipped while decorating the tree with her parents, of carols sung off-key but with heart, of laughter shared with friends and neighbors.

Lauren slowed the car, allowing herself to drink in the sight of the elaborate Christmas display outside the school. "Oh, Mama would love to see this," she said aloud, making a mental note to bring her parents here later.

As she turned onto Maple Avenue, the scent of freshly baked gingerbread wafted through the air, transporting her back to countless Christmas Eves spent in her mother's kitchen. Lauren's stomach growled in response, and she smiled.

The familiar houses lining the street tugged at her heartstrings. Each one held a story, a memory. There was the Johnsons' place, where she and her best friend Mary had built countless snowmen. And the Wilsons' house, with its grand porch where they'd held impromptu caroling sessions.

Lauren's chest tightened with a bittersweet ache. *I've missed this so much*, she thought. *Why did I stay away for so long?*

As she approached her childhood home, Lauren felt a mix of excitement and nervousness bubbling up inside her. The house looked just as she remembered—the wreath on the door, the soft glow of candlelight in the windows, the smoke curling from the chimney.

Well, here goes nothing. Lauren took a deep breath as she pulled into the driveway. *Time to face the music—and Mama's infamous interrogations about my love life.*

With a gentle laugh, she stepped out of the car, the crunch of snow beneath her boots a welcome sound. The porch light flickered on, and Lauren's heart swelled with love and anticipation.

"Home," she breathed, "I'm finally home."

Lauren stepped onto the porch, her heart racing as she raised her hand to knock. Before her knuckles could touch the wood, the door swung open, revealing her mother's beaming face.

"Lauren, sweetheart!" her mother exclaimed,

pulling her into a warm embrace. "Oh, how we've missed you!"

The scent of cinnamon enveloped Lauren as she hugged her mother back. "I've missed you too, Mama," she said, her voice muffled against her mother's shoulder.

As they pulled apart, Lauren's father appeared behind her mother, his eyes twinkling. "There's our city girl," he said with a chuckle. "Come on in before you freeze out there."

Lauren stepped inside, the warmth of the house washing over her. The living room was adorned with twinkling lights and garlands, the Christmas tree standing proud in the corner. Memories flooded back, bringing a lump to her throat.

"It's perfect," she whispered, taking it all in. "Just like I remember."

Her mother squeezed her hand. "We've been waiting all day to hear about your big city adventures. How's that fancy marketing job treating you?"

Lauren's smile faltered slightly. "It's...challenging," she admitted, sinking onto the familiar plush sofa. "Sometimes I wonder if I made the right choice, moving away."

Her father settled into his armchair, leaning

forward. "Now, now, pumpkin. Remember what we always say in this family?"

Lauren couldn't help but grin. "God has a plan for everything," they recited in unison, laughing.

As the evening wore on, they shared stories and laughter, the warmth of family wrapping around Lauren like a cozy blanket. She found herself relaxing, the stress of city life melting away.

It was good to be home.

The next morning, Lauren decided to grab breakfast at Milly's Diner, a local favorite. As she settled into a booth, the aroma of fresh coffee and syrupy pancakes filled the air.

"Well, if it isn't Lauren Beard!" Milly herself called out, bustling over with a pot of coffee. "Home for the holidays, sugar?"

Lauren nodded, smiling. "Yep."

As Milly poured her coffee, Lauren couldn't help but overhear the conversation from the next booth.

"Did you hear about that new fella in town?" a familiar voice gossiped. "Shane something-or-other. Moved into old Mrs. Peterson's place."

Lauren's ears perked up, her curiosity piqued despite herself.

"Oh, I saw him at the grocery store," another voice chimed in. "Handsome as can be, but awfully quiet. Wonder what his story is?"

Lauren sipped her coffee, her mind whirling with questions about this mysterious newcomer. She caught herself and shook her head, chuckling softly. Some things really didn't change—small town gossip was alive and well.

But who was she to talk? She was here all of one day and she was already feeding into it too.

She stirred her coffee absently, her mind still buzzing with thoughts of the enigmatic Shane Fisher. The chatter of the diner faded into background noise as she found herself lost in contemplation.

"Penny for your thoughts?" Milly's voice cut through her reverie.

Lauren looked up, a sheepish smile playing on her lips. "Oh, just...thinking about how some things never change around here."

Milly chuckled, refilling Lauren's cup. "Like our fondness for a good mystery, you mean?"

"Exactly," Lauren replied, her eyes twinkling. "So, what's your take on this Shane character?"

Milly leaned in conspiratorially. "Well, he's been coming in for breakfast most mornings. Always orders the same thing—black coffee and wheat toast. Scribbles in this tattered old journal of his."

Lauren's marketing instincts kicked in. "A writer, maybe?"

"Could be," Milly nodded. "Though what brings a writer to our little town is beyond me."

Lauren's gaze drifted to the frost-covered window, watching as early morning shoppers bustled along the sidewalk. "Maybe he's looking for inspiration," she mused, more to herself than to Milly.

As she turned back, Lauren caught sight of a tall figure entering the diner. His disheveled dark hair was dusted with snowflakes, and he carried himself with a quiet confidence that immediately drew her attention.

"Well, speak of the devil," Milly whispered, straightening up. "That's him now."

Lauren's heart skipped a beat as she watched Shane Fisher make his way to the counter, his piercing blue eyes scanning the room briefly before settling on an empty stool. She found herself wondering what stories those eyes held, what had brought him to this small corner of Virginia.

And that's when he looked up and his eyes met hers.

Lauren couldn't quite stop her gasp. He stared at her so intently, it was like he was looking right through her.

Her face colored and she looked back down at her coffee, her heart thumping.

When she finally got the courage to look back up, he was gone.

Shane something-or-other was a mystery indeed.

Chapter Two

Lauren smoothed her skirt as she slid into the familiar wooden pew, the scent of lemon polish and hymnals filling her senses. Her mother gave her hand a gentle squeeze before turning her attention to Pastor Roberts at the pulpit. As Lauren's gaze swept across the congregation, a flicker of movement caught her eye.

There, in the back row, was Shane. His dark, tousled hair and scruffy beard stood out among the neatly pressed suits and floral dresses. Lauren found herself once again wondering about the newcomer, her mind drifting from the sermon.

Who *was* he?

As the final notes of "Amazing Grace" faded away, Lauren stood with the rest of the congregation. She couldn't help but glance back at the mystery man, only to find his piercing blue eyes meeting hers. A warm smile tugged at the corners of his mouth, and Lauren felt her cheeks flush as she quickly looked away.

"Earth to Lauren," her sister whispered, nudging her with an elbow. "You coming?"

Lauren blinked, realizing she'd been lost in thought. "Oh, right. Sorry."

As they filed out of the pews, Lauren's heart raced with each step closer to the back of the church. She found herself hoping for a chance to speak with the newcomer, even if just to say hello.

To her surprise and delight, he was still there, lingering by the exit. Up close, Lauren noticed the soft, worn fabric of his flannel shirt and the way his eyes crinkled at the corners when he smiled.

"Hi there," Lauren said, summoning her courage. "I don't think we've met before. I'm Lauren Beard."

The man's smile widened, revealing a warmth that seemed to radiate from within. "Shane Fisher," he replied, his voice a gentle rumble. "It's nice to meet you, Lauren."

Fisher. That was his last name.

As they shook hands, Lauren felt a spark of connection. There was something about Shane's presence that put her at ease, despite the butterflies in her stomach.

"First time visiting our church?" Lauren asked, genuinely curious.

Shane nodded. "Just moved to town, actually. About a month ago. Thought I'd check it out. Though, I've seen nearly all these people around town, but I didn't see you until yesterday."

Lauren's heart glowed. *He remembered her.* "Well, I live in the city, actually. I'm just home for the holidays."

"Ah," he nodded.

As they exchanged a few more pleasantries, Lauren found herself captivated by Shane's gentle demeanor and the way he seemed to listen intently to every word she said. It was as if, for those few moments, they were the only two people in the world.

Lauren tucked a strand of chestnut hair behind her ear, curiosity piquing. "So, what brings you to Virginia? Are you here for work?"

Shane's blue eyes lit up, a hint of excitement breaking through his calm demeanor. "I'm a writer, actually. I came here seeking inspiration for my next novel."

Lauren's heart skipped a beat. "A writer? That's fascinating! What kind of stories do you write?"

Shane rubbed his scruffy beard thoughtfully. "I dabble in various genres, but I'm drawn to stories of redemption and second chances. There's something about small towns that seems to nurture those themes."

Lauren nodded enthusiastically. "I couldn't agree more. Have you read any Marilynne Robinson? Her 'Gilead' series captures that small-town essence beautifully."

Shane's eyes widened in surprise and delight. "Absolutely! Robinson's prose is like a warm embrace. I'm particularly fond of 'Home.'"

As they delved deeper into their literary discussion, Lauren felt a connection blossoming. She found herself gesturing animatedly as she spoke, her usual overthinking giving way to genuine excitement.

"You know," Shane said, a soft smile playing on his lips, "I was worried about finding kindred spirits here. It's refreshing to meet someone who shares my passion for literature."

Lauren's cheeks warmed at the compliment. "Well, we're not all about football and sweet tea down here," she quipped, earning a chuckle from Shane.

As they continued to chat, Lauren couldn't help but marvel at how easy it felt to talk to Shane. His quiet confidence and thoughtful responses drew her in. He was really easy to talk to.

Lauren glanced at her watch, surprised at how quickly time had passed. The warm afternoon sunlight streamed through the church windows, casting a golden glow on Shane's thoughtful face. She felt a sudden urge to prolong their conversation.

"Shane," she said, her voice tinged with warmth, "I don't know if you have plans this evening, but we're having a community dinner at the town hall. It's nothing fancy, just good food and friendly faces. Would you like to join us?"

Lauren held her breath, realizing how much she wanted him to say yes. She watched as Shane's blue eyes lit up with interest.

"That sounds wonderful," he replied, his voice soft but eager. "I'd be honored to attend. To be honest, I've been looking for ways to immerse myself in the community. It's all part of the writing process, you know?"

Lauren beamed, her enthusiasm bubbling over. "Great! It starts at six. I can introduce you to some of the locals—they're full of stories that might spark your inspiration."

As they made plans to meet at the town hall, Lauren felt a flutter of excitement in her chest. She found herself looking forward to spending more time with this intriguing newcomer, even as a small voice in the back of her mind whispered cautions about getting too attached.

"I'll see you there," Shane said, offering a warm smile that made Lauren's heart skip a beat. "Thank you for the invitation, Lauren. It means more than you know."

Chapter Three

Lauren's fork clinked against her plate as she set it down, her laughter mingling with the cheerful chatter filling the community center. She turned to Shane, her eyes bright with amusement. "I can't believe you actually tried to roast marshmallows over a candle," she said, shaking her head. "How old were you?"

Shane's lips quirked into a sheepish grin, his blue eyes twinkling. "Twelve. In my defense, it was a really big candle."

"And how did that work out for you?" Lauren leaned in, genuinely curious.

"Let's just say I learned a valuable lesson about fire safety and patience," Shane chuckled, running a hand through his disheveled hair.

Lauren found herself drawn to the way his eyes crinkled at the corners when he laughed. There was something both familiar and mysterious about him that intrigued her. She took a sip of her hot cocoa, savoring the warmth that spread through her chest.

"So, what about you?" Shane asked, his voice soft and inviting. "Any childhood misadventures you'd care to share?"

Lauren hesitated for a moment, her mind drifting back to her younger years. "Well, there was this one time I convinced my little sister that if we scattered birdseed in the backyard, we'd grow a forest of lollipop trees."

Shane's eyebrows shot up. "And did she buy it?"

"Hook, line, and sinker," Lauren grinned. "We spent an entire afternoon 'planting' our future candy forest."

As they continued to swap stories, Lauren felt a sense of ease settle over her. It was refreshing to talk to someone who seemed genuinely interested in what she had to say, without the pressure of work deadlines or city expectations.

"You know," Shane said, glancing out the window at the snow-covered landscape, "this view never gets old. There's something magical about Virginia in the winter."

Lauren followed his gaze, her heart swelling with pride for her hometown. "It really is beautiful, isn't it? Have you had a chance to explore the hiking trails yet?"

Shane's eyes lit up. "I've been meaning to, but I haven't gotten around to it. Are you a hiker?"

"Am I ever!" Lauren exclaimed, her enthusiasm bubbling over. "There's this trail that leads to the most breathtaking overlook. The way the sun hits the valley on a clear winter morning...it's like something out of a painting."

As Lauren described her favorite spots, she noticed Shane listening intently, occasionally jotting down notes in his weathered journal. She wondered what stories those pages held, what worlds he was creating with his writer's imagination.

"You'll have to show me sometime," Shane said, his voice holding a note of hope. "I'd love to see it through your eyes."

Lauren felt a flutter in her chest at the suggestion. "I'd like that," she replied softly, surprised by how much she meant it.

As the evening wore on, Lauren found herself lost in conversation with Shane, the rest of the world fading into a comfortable background hum. For the first time in a long while, she felt truly present, not worrying about the future or second-guessing her choices. Instead, she simply enjoyed the moment, grateful for the unexpected connection she'd found in the most familiar of places.

A sudden gust of wind rattled the windows, drawing Lauren's attention away from Shane. She peered outside, her eyes widening at the swirling white that had engulfed the town.

"Oh my goodness," Lauren gasped, pressing her hand against the cold glass. "Where did this storm come from?"

Shane joined her at the window, his brow furrowed. "It wasn't in the forecast. Looks like Mother Nature had other plans."

As if on cue, the lights flickered once, twice, and then plunged the room into darkness. A chorus of surprised exclamations rose from the gathered townspeople.

Lauren's leadership instincts kicked in immediately. "Everyone stay calm," she called out, her voice steady and reassuring. "Let's get some candles lit."

She fumbled in her purse for her phone, using its flashlight to navigate through the dim room. Shane was right behind her, his presence a comforting warmth at her back.

"I've got some emergency supplies in my car," he

offered. "Flashlights, batteries, the works. Old habits from my camping days."

Lauren couldn't help but smile. "A writer and a Boy Scout. You're full of surprises, Shane Fisher."

As they worked to illuminate the room, Lauren's mind raced with possibilities. "We can't send everyone home in this weather," she mused aloud. "My family's house isn't far. It's got a generator and plenty of space."

Shane nodded, already catching on to her train of thought. "A makeshift shelter. That's brilliant, Lauren. How can I help?"

"Can you start organizing carpools? I'll call my parents and let them know we're coming."

As Lauren dialed her mother's number, she couldn't help but feel a surge of excitement beneath her concern. This was what she loved about her hometown—the way everyone came together in times of need. And having Shane by her side, his quiet confidence bolstering her own, made her feel like they could handle anything the storm threw their way.

"Mom?" she said as the call connected. "We've got a situation here. How do you feel about hosting an impromptu blizzard party?"

❄

The warm glow of candlelight flickered across Lauren's face as she watched Shane regale their impromptu guests with a story from his latest writing adventure. His eyes sparkled with animation, his hands gesturing expressively as he spoke. Lauren found herself drawn in, not just by the tale, but by the storyteller himself.

"And there I was," Shane chuckled, "stuck in a tiny Tibetan village with no WiFi and a looming deadline. Talk about a writer's nightmare!"

The room erupted in laughter, and Lauren felt a warmth spread through her chest that had nothing to do with the steaming mug of cocoa in her hands. She marveled at how effortlessly Shane had integrated himself into their close-knit community, his quiet confidence and genuine interest in others drawing people to him like moths to a flame.

As the laughter died down, Lauren caught Shane's eye across the room. He gave her a soft smile that made her heart skip a beat. She found herself wondering, not for the first time that evening, what it would be like to be the subject of one of his stories.

"You've got quite a knack for this," Lauren said, moving closer to him as the group broke into smaller conversations. "I don't think I've ever seen Mrs. Holloway warm up to someone so quickly."

Shane's eyes crinkled at the corners as he smiled. "It's easy when you're surrounded by such wonderful people. Your hometown is something special, Lauren."

Lauren felt a familiar pang of uncertainty. "It is," she agreed, her voice softening. "Sometimes I wonder if I made the right choice, leaving for the city."

Shane regarded her thoughtfully. "Yeah, I know what you mean. It's easy to question our choices, but I bet you carry a piece of this place with you wherever you go."

His words settled over Lauren like a warm blanket, easing a tension she hadn't realized she'd been carrying. In that moment, amidst the gentle flicker of candles and the soft murmur of conversation, Lauren felt a profound sense of peace wash over her. She realized that it wasn't just the comfort of home, but Shane's presence that made her feel so at ease.

Chapter Four

Lauren's breath formed delicate clouds in the crisp winter air as she turned to Shane, her eyes sparkling with excitement. "Hey, what do you say we take a walk in the park? The fresh snow looks absolutely magical."

Shane's blue eyes lit up, a smile tugging at the corners of his mouth. "That sounds perfect. I could use some inspiration for my writing, and there's nothing quite like a winter wonderland to stir the imagination."

As they strolled into the park, Lauren marveled at the pristine blanket of snow covering the landscape. The bare branches of the trees were adorned with a glistening frost, creating a scene straight out of a fairy tale. She couldn't help but feel a childlike wonder bubbling up inside her.

"You know," Lauren said, her voice soft and reminiscent, "this reminds me of the winters in New York. The city might be busy, bit it has the most beautiful snowfalls."

Shane tilted his head, intrigued. "Tell me more about your life in New York. If you don't mind, of course."

Lauren smiled, her eyes taking on a wistful gleam as memories flooded her mind. "Well, I moved there for my career in marketing. It was a dream come true, working for a big firm and being part of the hustle and bustle. But as much as I love the energy of the city, I always find myself longing for the warmth and simplicity of my hometown during the holidays."

Shane nodded, understanding etched on his features. "I can relate to that feeling. Sometimes, in the pursuit of our dreams, we find ourselves far from the things that ground us. It's important to hold onto those roots, even as we grow and change."

Lauren looked at him, a newfound appreciation in her eyes. "That's so true. It's like we're constantly trying to find a balance between who we were and who we're becoming.

As they walked, their footsteps crunching in the

snow, Lauren found herself opening up more. "I've always dreamed of bringing that small-town magic to the city somehow. Maybe through event planning or community outreach."

Shane nodded thoughtfully, his writer's mind clearly at work. "That's beautiful, Lauren." He paused, then added with a hint of vulnerability, "I've always wanted to capture that kind of warmth and connection in my writing."

Lauren felt a flutter in her chest at his openness. "What about you, Shane? What are your dreams beyond writing?"

He gazed at the snow-covered path ahead, his expression pensive. "I want my stories to touch people's lives, to remind them of the beauty in everyday moments. But more than that, I hope to find a place where I truly belong."

As they continued their walk, sharing hopes and aspirations, Lauren couldn't help but feel a growing connection with Shane. The winter wonderland around them seemed to fade into the background as their conversation deepened, drawing them closer with each step through the freshly fallen snow.

Lauren was full of curiosity as Shane's words hung in the crisp winter air. "Finding a place to belong...I can relate to that," she said softly. "But tell me, what's been your biggest challenge as a writer?"

Shane's piercing blue eyes met hers, a flicker of vulnerability passing through them. "Honestly? Self-doubt," he admitted, running a hand through his disheveled dark hair. "Some days, the words flow like a river. Other days..." He trailed off, his gaze drifting to the snow-laden trees.

Lauren felt a surge of empathy. "Those are the days when the blank page seems terrifying, right?"

He nodded, a small smile tugging at his lips. "Exactly. It's like the inspiration just...vanishes."

"But you keep going," Lauren said, her voice warm with encouragement. "That takes real strength, Shane."

His smile widened slightly. "Thanks, Lauren. It means a lot to hear that."

As they rounded a bend in the path, Lauren's eyes lit up. "Hey, want to build a snowman? Might help spark some creativity!"

Shane chuckled, his earlier tension melting away. "Why not? I haven't done that since I was a kid."

They set to work, rolling snow and laughing as they shaped their frosty creation. Lauren packed snow onto the middle section, her cheeks flushed from the cold and exertion. "You know," she said, patting the snowman's belly, "sometimes the best ideas come when you're not actively chasing them."

Shane nodded, carefully placing pebbles for the snowman's eyes. "You're right. Maybe I need to let go a little, have more fun like this."

Suddenly, a snowball hit Shane squarely in the chest. He looked up to see Lauren grinning mischievously, another snowball already in hand. "Oh, it's on!" he declared, scooping up snow.

Soon, the air was filled with flying snowballs and peals of laughter. As Lauren ducked behind a tree, she felt a warmth in her chest that had nothing to do with physical exertion. There was something about Shane—his quiet depth, his vulnerability—that drew her in, making her feel more alive than she had in years.

Lauren leaned against the tree, catching her breath. Her heart raced, but not just from the snowball fight. She watched Shane brushing snow from his beard, his blue eyes twinkling with mirth, and felt a flutter in her stomach.

"Truce?" Shane called out, holding up his hands in mock surrender.

"Truce," Lauren agreed, emerging from her hiding spot. She walked towards him, suddenly aware of how close they were standing. "That was fun. I haven't played like that in ages."

Shane smiled, a warm, genuine expression that made Lauren's breath catch. "Me neither. Thanks for reminding me how to have a good time."

Lauren tucked a loose strand of hair behind her ear, her mind whirling. "I'm glad," she said softly. "You know, Shane, I've really enjoyed getting to know you today."

"The feeling's mutual," Shane replied, his gaze holding hers.

Lauren's heart skipped a beat. She wanted to say more, to explore this new, exciting feeling, but uncertainty held her back. Instead, she glanced at her watch. "Oh, wow. I didn't realize how late it's gotten. We should probably head back."

As they walked side by side, their arms occasionally brushing, Lauren found herself stealing glances at Shane. She thought, *What am I doing? I barely know him. But there's just something about him...*

"Everything okay?" Shane asked, noticing her distraction.

Lauren nodded, forcing a smile. "Just thinking

about how nice today has been." She paused, then added, "Maybe we could do this again sometime?"

Shane's face lit up. "I'd like that."

As they neared the end of the park, Lauren's mind raced. She was developing feelings for Shane, that much was clear. But how to proceed? Should she be more direct? Take it slow? The uncertainty was both thrilling and terrifying.

Chapter Five

Lauren's eyes sparkled as she spotted Shane across the town square, his tousled dark hair catching the soft glow of the holiday lights. Her heart quickened as she waved him over, a warm smile spreading across her face.

"Shane! I'm so glad I ran into you," she called out, her breath visible in the crisp winter air.

He approached with his usual quiet grace, a hint of curiosity in his piercing blue eyes. "Lauren, what a pleasant surprise. How are you?"

She clasped her gloved hands together, barely containing her excitement. "I'm wonderful, thank you. Listen, I have an idea I wanted to run by you. The local community center is hosting a charity event this weekend to help families in need for the holidays. I was wondering if you'd like to volunteer with me?"

Shane's expression softened, a small smile tugging at the corners of his mouth. "That sounds like a worthy cause. What would we be doing?"

Lauren's mind raced with possibilities. This could be the perfect opportunity to spend more time with Shane and see a different side of him.

"We'd be wrapping gifts, organizing food donations, that sort of thing," she explained, her voice warm with enthusiasm. "It's a chance to give back to the community and spread some holiday cheer. What do you say?"

Shane nodded, his eyes twinkling with interest. "I'd be honored to join you, Lauren. It might even inspire some new story ideas."

The day of the event arrived, and Lauren found herself standing beside Shane in the bustling community center. The air was filled with the scent of cinnamon and the sound of cheerful chatter. They settled at a gift-wrapping station, surrounded by colorful paper and ribbons.

"I have to warn you," Shane said with a wry smile as he picked up a roll of wrapping paper, "I'm not known for my gift-wrapping skills."

Lauren laughed, the sound light and melodious.

"Don't worry, I'll teach you my secret techniques. By the end of the day, you'll be a pro."

As they worked side by side, Lauren couldn't help but steal glances at Shane. His brow furrowed in concentration as he carefully folded the paper around a toy truck, his long fingers deftly creasing the edges.

"You're a natural," she encouraged, feeling a warmth spread through her chest at the sight of his proud smile.

They fell into a comfortable rhythm, chatting and laughing as they wrapped gift after gift. Lauren found herself captivated by Shane's quiet humor and thoughtful observations about the holiday season.

"You know," Shane mused as he tied a bow on a beautifully wrapped package, "there's something magical about giving anonymously. It's like being a secret Santa for an entire community."

Lauren nodded, her heart swelling with affection. "I couldn't agree more. It's not about recognition. It's about spreading joy and hope."

As they moved on to organizing food donations, Lauren couldn't help but feel a sense of purpose and contentment. Working alongside Shane, their hands occasionally brushing as they sorted canned goods, she realized that this simple act of volunteering was bringing them closer in ways she hadn't anticipated.

The day flew by in a flurry of activity, and before they knew it, the event was winding down. Lauren looked around at the mountains of wrapped gifts and neatly organized food boxes, a sense of accomplishment washing over her.

"We make quite a team," she said softly, turning to Shane with a warm smile.

He met her gaze, his blue eyes filled with a mixture of gratitude and something deeper that made Lauren's heart skip a beat. "Indeed we do, Lauren. Thank you for inviting me. This has been...unexpectedly wonderful."

As Lauren and Shane stood near the charity event's exit, a commotion caught their attention. A family of five—a weary-looking mother, a father with calloused hands, and three wide-eyed children—approached the gift distribution area.

"Oh, Shane, look," Lauren whispered, gently touching his arm.

They watched as volunteers presented the family with carefully wrapped gifts and a large box of food. The youngest child, a girl no older than five, squealed with delight as she was handed a soft, plush teddy bear.

"Mommy, look! It's just like the one in the store window!" the little girl exclaimed, hugging the bear tightly.

Shane's breath caught in his throat, and Lauren noticed his eyes glistening. The parents, overwhelmed with gratitude, embraced each other as tears streamed down their faces.

"I can't believe this," the mother said, her voice thick with emotion. "You've made our Christmas possible. Thank you, thank you so much."

Lauren felt a lump form in her throat. She glanced at Shane, who was furiously scribbling in his weathered journal.

"Are you okay?" she asked softly.

Shane nodded, closing his journal. "Yeah, I just...This reminds me of something from my past."

"Would you like to share?" Lauren prompted gently.

Shane took a deep breath, his piercing blue eyes meeting hers. "When I was a kid, my family went through a rough patch. One Christmas, we didn't have much, but a local charity provided gifts for us. I got a notebook and a set of pens—it was the start of my writing journey."

Lauren listened intently, touched by his vulnerability.

"That act of kindness changed my life," Shane continued, his voice low and reflective. "It taught me the power of generosity and gratitude. I've tried to pay it forward ever since."

Lauren felt a warm rush of affection. "Shane, that's beautiful. Thank you for sharing that with me."

He gave her a small, genuine smile. "Thank you for bringing me here today. It's reminded me of what really matters."

As they watched the family leave, arms full of gifts and hearts full of joy, Lauren realized that this experience had deepened her connection with Shane in ways she never expected.

Chapter Six

The warm glow of candles illuminated Lauren's face as she entered the cozy workshop, her eyes widening with delight. The scent of beeswax and cinnamon filled the air, instantly transporting her back to childhood Christmases. She spotted Shane near the back, his tousled dark hair catching the flickering light.

"There you are," Lauren said, making her way over. "I was worried I'd be the only one here without an artistic bone in my body."

Shane looked up from his notebook, a small smile playing at his lips. "I wouldn't be too sure about that. My artistic skills begin and end with stick figures."

Lauren laughed, feeling some of her nervousness

dissipate. As they settled into their workstation, she couldn't help but notice how at ease Shane seemed, despite being new in town. She wondered what stories were hidden behind those piercing blue eyes.

"So, what kind of candle are you thinking of making?" Lauren asked, fingering the various molds and decorations laid out before them.

Shane rubbed his scruffy beard thoughtfully. "I'm thinking something that captures the essence of this town. Maybe pine and cinnamon?"

"Ooh, that sounds perfect," Lauren nodded enthusiastically. "I'm leaning towards vanilla and cranberry myself. Reminds me of baking with my grandmother."

As they began pouring their wax, Lauren found herself relaxing into the process. She stole glances at Shane, noticing the careful way he measured each ingredient, his brow furrowed in concentration.

"You know," Shane said, breaking the comfortable silence, "I think I might use this experience in my next book. A romance in a candle shop could be interesting."

Lauren's eyes lit up. "Oh, that would be lovely! I can just imagine it now—two people bonding over shared scents and memories."

Shane chuckled, a warm sound that sent a flutter

through Lauren's chest. "Exactly. Though I doubt my characters would be as clumsy as I am with this wax."

As if on cue, a glob of wax spilled onto the table. They both burst into laughter, Shane's quieter and Lauren's more exuberant.

"Here," Lauren said, still giggling as she handed him a cloth. "Let me help you clean that up."

Their hands brushed as she passed him the cloth, and Lauren felt a spark of electricity. She wondered if Shane felt it too, but his face remained impassive, save for the slight crinkle around his eyes.

As they moved on to decorating their candles, Lauren found herself opening up about her marketing job in the city. "It's exciting work, but sometimes I miss the simplicity of small-town life," she admitted, carefully placing a sprig of holly on her candle.

Shane nodded, his eyes understanding. "I can relate to that. There's something special about places like this, where time seems to slow down and people really connect."

Lauren felt a warmth spread through her chest, not just from the candles surrounding them, but from Shane's words.

Lauren smiled warmly, her fingers tracing the

edge of her candle. "You know, this reminds me so much of the Christmases from my childhood. We had this tradition where my mom, dad, and I would make ornaments together every year."

Shane's blue eyes sparkled with interest. "That sounds wonderful. What kind of ornaments?"

"Oh, all sorts," Lauren replied, her voice filled with nostalgia. "One year it was pinecone elves, another year we made little stuffed gingerbread men. What about you? Did your family have any special holiday customs?"

A shadow crossed Shane's face, but he managed a small smile. "We did, actually. Every Christmas Eve, we'd drive around town looking at the lights. Then we'd come home and read 'The Night Before Christmas' together."

Lauren noticed the past tense and felt a pang of concern. "That sounds lovely, Shane. Do you still keep up the tradition?"

Shane's fingers stilled on his candle, his voice growing softer. "I...I haven't for a while now. My parents were taken from me in a car crash years ago."

Lauren's heart clenched, her hand instinctively reaching out to touch Shane's arm. "Oh, Shane, I'm so sorry. That must have been devastating."

Shane nodded, his eyes meeting hers with a mix

of sadness and gratitude. "It was. But you know, God has been my comfort through it all. His presence has been my light in the darkest times."

Lauren felt a surge of warmth and connection. "I understand completely. My faith has been my anchor too, especially when I'm feeling lost or uncertain about my future."

"It's amazing how faith can guide us, isn't it?" Shane said, his voice growing stronger. "Even when we can't see the path ahead clearly."

As they continued working on their candles, Lauren felt a deeper bond forming between them, built on shared values and mutual understanding. The flickering candlelight seemed to mirror the spark of connection growing between them, promising warmth and light in the days to come.

The workshop was winding down, and Lauren carefully lifted her finished candle, a delicate creation adorned with pine sprigs and cinnamon sticks. Shane's candle stood next to hers, its rustic charm complementing her more intricate design.

"Shall we light them?" Shane asked, his blue eyes twinkling in the dim light of the workshop.

Lauren nodded, a shy smile playing on her lips. "Together?"

They each took a match, striking them simultaneously. The small flames danced to life, and they gently touched them to their candle wicks. As the flames caught, a warm glow enveloped them, casting soft shadows across their faces.

Lauren inhaled deeply, the scent of vanilla and cinnamon filling her senses. "It's beautiful," she murmured, her gaze fixed on the flickering light.

Shane's voice was low and gentle when he replied, "It really is. Reminds me of the power of small lights in dark places."

Lauren glanced up at him, twirling a strand of hair around her finger. "What do you mean?"

"Well," Shane began, his hand absently reaching for his journal, "I've been thinking about how a single candle can illuminate a whole room. It's like faith, or hope...or even love. Just a spark can change everything."

Lauren felt her heart skip a beat. "That's...that's a beautiful way to look at it."

They fell into a comfortable silence, the soft glow of their candles creating an intimate bubble around them. Lauren found herself studying Shane's face, noticing how the flickering light softened his features, making him look younger and more vulnerable.

"Lauren," Shane said suddenly, his voice barely above a whisper, "I'm really glad I came here—to this town. Meeting you...it's been like finding a light I didn't know I was missing."

Lauren's breath caught in her throat. She wanted to respond, to tell him how she felt the same way, but the words seemed to stick. Instead, she reached out and gently squeezed his hand, hoping her touch could convey what her voice couldn't.

As their fingers intertwined, Lauren realized that maybe, just maybe, she had found her own guiding light in the most unexpected place.

Chapter Seven

The aroma of cinnamon and pine wafted through the Beard family home as Lauren opened the front door, revealing Shane standing on the porch with a nervous smile. His scruffy beard was neatly trimmed, and he'd swapped his usual worn sweater for a crisp button-down shirt.

"Shane! You made it," Lauren beamed, her heart fluttering. She gestured for him to come inside. "Welcome to our little Christmas haven."

Lauren had invited him to her family's home since he was all alone in town.

As Shane stepped in, Lauren's mother emerged from the kitchen, wiping flour-dusted hands on her festive apron. "You must be Shane," she said warmly. "We're so glad you could join us."

Lauren watched as Shane's tense shoulders relaxed slightly. He offered a small, grateful nod. "Thank you for having me, Mrs. Beard. It smells wonderful in here."

Lauren's father appeared, his booming laugh filling the room. "Hope you brought your appetite, son! We've got enough food to feed an army."

Lauren felt a rush of affection for her parents' immediate acceptance of Shane. She caught his eye and gave an encouraging smile, silently communicating that he was welcome here.

"Lauren, why don't you show Shane around while we finish up in the kitchen?" her mother suggested, a knowing twinkle in her eye.

As Lauren led Shane through the living room, she noticed him taking in the twinkling lights, handmade ornaments, and childhood photos adorning the mantle. His writer's gaze seemed to absorb every detail.

"This is beautiful," Shane murmured, pausing to admire a faded photograph of a young Lauren building a snowman. "Your family really embraces the spirit of the season."

Lauren felt a warmth spread through her chest. "Christmas has always been special for us," she explained, her voice soft with nostalgia. "Every ornament, every tradition has a story behind it."

She watched as Shane's expression softened, a hint of wistfulness in his eyes.

"Well," she said brightly, pushing away the moment of melancholy, "let me show you our pride and joy—the Christmas tree!"

As they moved towards the twinkling centerpiece of the room, Lauren felt Shane's hand brush against hers. The brief contact sent a thrill through her, and she found herself hoping that this Christmas might mark the beginning of a new tradition—one that included Shane.

Lauren's heart fluttered as she reached for the carefully wrapped gift she'd stuck beneath the tree. She turned to Shane, a shy smile playing on her lips. "I hope you like it," she said, handing him the package.

Shane's blue eyes sparkled with curiosity as he carefully unwrapped the present. His face lit up as he revealed a leather-bound journal, its cover embossed with intricate designs.

"Lauren, this is...incredible," he breathed, running his fingers over the soft leather. "How did you know?"

She laughed softly, tucking a strand of chestnut

hair behind her ear. "I may have noticed your old journal looking a bit worse for wear. I thought you might need a new one for your next bestseller."

Shane's gaze met hers, filled with warmth and gratitude. "Thank you. This means more than you know." He paused, then reached into his coat pocket. "I have something for you too."

Lauren's eyes widened as Shane presented her with a small, velvet box. Inside was a delicate silver charm bracelet, adorned with tiny snowflakes.

"Oh, Shane," she whispered, her voice thick with emotion. "It's beautiful."

“To commemorate our time playing in the snow like children.” He grinned at her, and she grinned back.

“It’s perfect.”

As Shane helped her fasten the bracelet, Lauren felt a surge of affection for this thoughtful man who had come to mean so much to her in such a short time.

Their moment was interrupted by Diane's cheerful call from the dining room. "Dinner's ready, everyone!"

As they made their way to the table, Lauren couldn't help but marvel at how seamlessly Shane seemed to fit into her family's celebrations. The dining room was aglow with candlelight, the table laden with traditional dishes that filled the air with mouthwatering aromas.

"So, Shane," Robert began as they settled into their seats, "Lauren tells us you're a writer. What inspired you to pursue that path?"

Shane smiled, his eyes meeting Lauren's briefly before he answered. "I've always been drawn to stories, Mr. Beard. There's something magical about creating worlds and characters that can touch people's lives."

"That's beautiful," Diane interjected, her eyes shining. "And do you find your faith plays a role in your writing?"

Lauren watched Shane carefully, curious about his response. He seemed to consider the question thoughtfully before answering.

"It does," he said slowly. "I believe that story-telling can be a powerful way to explore questions of faith and morality. My goal is to write stories that inspire hope and reflection."

As the conversation flowed, Lauren found herself drawn into a discussion about balancing career ambitions with personal life. "It's not always easy," she admitted, thinking of her own struggles. "But I believe that with faith and perseverance, it's possible to find that balance."

Shane nodded in agreement. "I've learned that success means different things to different people. For me, it's about creating meaningful work while nurturing the relationships that matter most."

Lauren felt a warmth spread through her chest at his words.

Her gaze drifted to the window, where snowflakes danced in the glow of the porch light. The laughter and chatter from the dining room faded into a pleasant hum as she turned to Shane, a mischievous glint in her eye.

"Want to sneak out for some fresh air?" she whispered, nudging his arm gently.

Shane's blue eyes sparkled with intrigue. "Lead the way," he murmured, a crooked smile playing on his lips.

They slipped out onto the porch, the cold air nipping at their cheeks. Lauren shivered, wrapping her arms around herself. Without a word, Shane shrugged off his coat and draped it over her shoulders.

"Such a gentleman," Lauren teased, breathing in the scent of pine and something uniquely Shane.

He chuckled softly, leaning against the porch

railing. "Just don't want you freezing on my account."

Lauren joined him, their shoulders barely touching. The silence between them felt comfortable, charged with unspoken potential.

"You know," Shane began, his voice low and thoughtful, "I haven't felt this...at peace in a long time."

Lauren's heart quickened. "Neither have I," she admitted, turning to face him. "It's like...coming home, but to a place I've never been before."

Shane's hand found hers, his touch sending tingles up her arm. "Lauren, I—"

The porch light flickered, startling them both. They laughed nervously, the moment suspended between them like a delicate ornament.

"You were saying?" Lauren prompted, her voice barely above a whisper.

Shane took a deep breath, his eyes never leaving hers. "I think I'm falling for you, Lauren Beard."

Lauren's breath caught in her throat, her heart pounding as Shane's words hung in the air between them. She searched his face, finding only sincerity and vulnerability in his piercing blue eyes.

"Shane, I..." She swallowed, her voice trembling slightly. "I think I'm falling for you too."

A slow, wonderstruck smile spread across Shane's face, his eyes crinkling at the corners. He reached up, gently brushing a stray lock of hair from her cheek. Lauren leaned into his touch, her skin tingling where his fingers grazed.

"I never expected to find someone like you," Shane murmured, his thumb tracing the curve of her cheekbone. "Someone who makes me feel like I belong."

Lauren's eyes filled with tears, her heart overflowing with emotion.

Slowly, tentatively, Shane leaned in, his lips a hairsbreadth from hers. Lauren's eyes fluttered closed as she bridged the gap, their lips meeting in a soft, tender kiss that held the promise of countless more to come.

When they parted, Lauren rested her forehead against his, a blissful smile playing on her lips. "Merry Christmas, Shane," she whispered.

"Merry Christmas, Lauren," he replied, his voice rough with emotion.

They stood there, wrapped in each other's arms, as the snow fell softly around them. In that moment, Lauren knew that this Christmas would be one she'd never forget—the Christmas that brought Shane into her life and into her heart.

From inside, the sound of laughter and clinking dishes drifted out to the porch, a reminder of the warmth and love waiting for them. Lauren laced her fingers through Shane's, giving his hand a gentle squeeze.

"Ready to head back in?" she asked, her eyes sparkling with joy.

Shane nodded, a contented smile on his face. "Lead the way."

Hand in hand, they stepped back into the house, the scent of cinnamon and pine enveloping them once more. As they joined her family around the fireplace, Lauren's heart swelled with gratitude for the precious gift she'd been given—the gift of love, faith, and a future filled with endless possibility.

Chapter Eight

Lauren's boots crunched through the fresh snow as she walked beside Shane, their breath forming misty clouds in the crisp midnight air. The town square glittered with twinkling lights, casting a warm glow on the blanket of white covering the ground.

"It's so peaceful out here," Lauren said softly, her eyes taking in the familiar sights of her hometown transformed into a winter wonderland. She felt a sense of calm wash over her, a stark contrast to the constant bustle of city life.

Shane nodded, his blue eyes reflecting the shimmer of Christmas lights. "There's something magical about a small town at night," he mused. "It's like the whole world has paused just for us."

Lauren's heart fluttered at his words. She sneaked a glance at his profile, admiring the way the light played on his scruffy beard. There was something about Shane that made her feel both excited and at ease, a combination she'd never experienced before.

As they strolled past the old gazebo, now draped in icicles, Shane cleared his throat. "So, Lauren," he began, his voice carrying a hint of hesitation, "have you given any thought to what comes next? After the holidays, I mean."

Lauren's stomach tightened. The question she'd been avoiding suddenly loomed large. "I...I'm not sure," she admitted, her voice barely above a whisper. "What about you? Will you stay here to finish your novel?"

Shane stopped walking and turned to face her, his expression earnest. "Actually, I wanted to talk to you about that. I know you have your life in the city, your career..." He paused, taking a deep breath. "But I want you to know that if you decide to go back, I'd be willing to go with you. Not saying that I don't think we could handle a long-distance relationship. It's just that life is too short, and I don't want to waste time being away from you."

Lauren's eyes widened in surprise as her heart melted at his words. "You would?"

He nodded, a gentle smile playing on his lips. "I can write from anywhere, Lauren. And the truth is, I just want to be with you."

Lauren's heart raced, a mix of joy and uncertainty swirling within her. The city, her job, her life there—it all seemed so distant now, standing here in the snow with Shane. She opened her mouth to respond, but found herself at a loss for words.

As they stood there, snowflakes began to fall gently around them, dusting Shane's dark hair with specks of white. Lauren reached out, brushing a flake from his cheek, her touch lingering for a moment.

"Shane, I..." she began, her voice trailing off as she searched for the right words to express the tumult of emotions inside her.

Lord, what do I do?

She felt a warm calm settle over her as she got her answer.

She knew what she was supposed to do.

Lauren took a deep breath, her warm exhale visible in the cold night air. She gazed into Shane's eyes, finding strength in their unwavering warmth.

"I don't want to go back to the city," she said softly, her voice barely above a whisper. "I want to stay here, in my hometown. Where we met."

Shane's face lit up with joy, but he remained silent, allowing her to continue.

"Being here these past few weeks, reconnecting with my roots, with you..." Lauren's voice trembled slightly. "It's made me realize what truly matters. The hustle of city life, the endless meetings and deadlines —they don't compare to the peace I feel right here, right now."

They resumed their walk, their steps slow and deliberate. Lauren's hand found Shane's, their fingers intertwining naturally.

"What about your job?" Shane asked gently, giving her hand a reassuring squeeze.

Lauren smiled, a newfound certainty in her eyes. "I can use my marketing skills anywhere. Maybe I'll start my own consultancy, help local businesses grow. Who knows? The possibilities are endless."

As they strolled beneath the twinkling stars, Lauren felt a sense of peace wash over her. She glanced at Shane, her heart swelling with affection.

"I've found something worth nurturing here," she said, her voice full of emotion. "A love I never expected, but one I can't imagine living without now."

Shane stopped walking, turning to face her. His

eyes shimmered in the starlight as he cupped her face gently with his free hand.

"Lauren," he whispered, his voice filled with awe and adoration.

Their lips met in a tender kiss, soft and sweet, yet filled with promise. As they parted, Lauren's eyes fluttered open, a radiant smile spreading across her face.

"So," Shane said, his voice playful. "Does this mean we're officially dating?"

Lauren laughed, the joyous sound echoing in the quiet night. "I'd say so, Mr. Novelist."

Lauren's laughter faded into a contented sigh as they resumed their walk, the crisp night air filled with possibility. She leaned her head against Shane's shoulder, reveling in the warmth of his presence.

"You know," Shane mused, his voice thoughtful, "I've been thinking about starting a writing group here in town. Maybe at the library or that cozy coffee shop on Main Street."

Lauren's eyes lit up. "That's a wonderful idea! I bet Cynthia would love to help organize it. She's always talking about wanting more cultural events in town."

Shane nodded, a smile playing on his lips. "And maybe we could work with your parents to host some events at the inn. Writing retreats or workshops?"

"Oh, Mom and Dad would adore that," Lauren said, her voice warm with affection. "Dad's always wanted to write his memoirs. This could be just the push he needs."

As they rounded the corner, the town's charming Christmas tree came into view, its twinkling lights a beacon of holiday cheer.

"You know," Lauren said, her voice soft with wonder, "I never thought I'd find my future here in my past. But now, I can't imagine it any other way."

Shane squeezed her hand. "Speaking of the future, what do you say we start a new Christmas tradition? Maybe volunteer at the shelter together?"

Lauren's heart swelled with love and gratitude. "I'd like that," she whispered, her voice thick with emotion. "I'd like that very much."

Excerpt from the next book in the A Very Merry State of Love series

CHRISTMAS IN MAINE

The snow-dusted pines whizzed by as Alexia Beasley's car wound its way down the familiar roads of her childhood. Her heart quickened with each passing landmark, memories of Christmases past flooding her mind. The old general store, now with a fresh coat of red paint, still had the same cheerful wreath on its door.

"Home sweet home," Alexia murmured, her breath fogging up the window. She couldn't help but smile as she turned onto Maple Street, where her parents' house stood proudly at the end of the cul-de-sac.

As she pulled into the driveway, the scent of pine and woodsmoke filled her nostrils. The two-story colonial was adorned with twinkling lights and garland, just as it had been every Christmas she could remember. Alexia's eyes misted over as she took in the sight, overwhelmed by a sense of belonging she hadn't felt in years.

The front door burst open before she could even cut the engine. Her mother rushed out, arms outstretched, with her father following close behind.

"Oh, sweetheart! You're here!" Marilyn exclaimed, enveloping Alexia in a warm embrace that smelled of cinnamon and vanilla.

"Hi, Mom," Alexia laughed, returning the hug fiercely. "Dad, a little help with the bags?"

Henry chuckled, his strong arms already reaching for her suitcases. "Welcome home, pumpkin. Your mother's been baking up a storm all day."

As they made their way inside, Alexia's gaze swept over the familiar entryway. The same wreath of pinecones hung on the wall, and the old grandfather clock in the corner still chimed every quarter-hour.

"Oh, honey, remember how you used to love helping me hang the stockings?" her mother said, gesturing to the fireplace mantel where four red stockings hung in a neat row.

Alexia nodded, a lump forming in her throat. "And Dad would always pretend he couldn't reach the top of the tree to let me put the star on."

Her father's eyes twinkled. "Well, now you're tall enough to do it without any help. Speaking of which, we've got the perfect tree waiting in the living room for you to decorate."

As they settled into the cozy living room, the scent of gingerbread wafted from the kitchen. Alexia sank into the soft cushions of the couch, letting the warmth of home and family wash over her.

"So, tell us all about the big city life," her mother said, settling in beside her daughter. "We want to hear everything."

Alexia smiled, realizing how much she'd missed this—the simple joy of being with her parents, sharing stories, and feeling completely at ease.

“Let her get unpacked first, Marilyn,” her father said with a chuckle.

Alexia gave her father a grateful smile as she headed to her room.

Once there, she unzipped her suitcase, the familiar scent of home mingling with the crisp winter air drifting through the cracked window. As she cleared out a dresser draw, she lifted out a stack of neatly folded sweaters and something small and glittery tumbled onto the patchwork quilt.

"Oh!" she exclaimed, picking up the delicate object. It was a hand-painted glass ornament, a miniature evergreen tree adorned with tiny gold stars. Alexia's breath caught in her throat as memories flooded back.

"I can't believe this is still here," she murmured, turning the ornament gently in her hands. Her mind drifted to Philip Bishop, the boy who had given her this ornament so many Christmases ago.

"Honey, everything okay up there?" her mother's voice called from downstairs.

"Yeah, Mom," Alexia replied, her voice slightly strained. "Just found an old ornament."

She set the ornament on her nightstand, her fingers lingering on its smooth surface. "I wonder what ever happened to you, Philip," she whispered.

Shaking off the wave of nostalgia, Alexia finished unpacking and decided to clear her head with a walk. She bundled up in her favorite peacoat and stepped out into the crisp afternoon air.

The woods behind her parents' house beckoned, a winter wonderland of snow-laden branches and hushed stillness. As Alexia crunched along the familiar path, she felt the tension in her shoulders begin to melt away.

"I'd forgotten how beautiful it is out here," she said softly, her breath forming little clouds in the frosty air. The only sounds were the crunch of snow beneath her boots and the occasional twitter of a brave winter bird.

Alexia paused in a small clearing, tilting her face up to catch a few errant snowflakes on her cheeks. A sense of peace washed over her, filling the empty spaces she hadn't even realized were there.

She closed her eyes and inhaling deeply. The scent of pine and winter air filled her lungs, grounding her in a way the bustling city never could.

As she stood there, Alexia felt a quiet certainty settle in her heart. Whatever challenges lay ahead, whatever decisions she faced, this place—these woods—would always be a part of her.

She continued walking, enjoying reconnecting with nature when she rounded a bend in the path and collided with a solid figure, letting out a startled "Oof!"

"Whoa there!" A deep, warm voice chuckled. "Are you okay?"

Alexia looked up, her eyes widening in recognition. "Philip? Philip Bishop?"

Philip's green eyes crinkled with surprise and delight. "Alexia Beasley? Is that really you?"

For a moment, they stood frozen, the years stretching between them like a chasm. Alexia's heart raced, a mix of awkwardness and excitement coursing through her.

"I...wow," she stammered, tucking a strand of hair behind her ear. "It's been so long."

Philip's easy smile broke the tension. "Too long. What brings you back to our winter wonderland?"

As they fell into step together, Alexia found herself relaxing. "Oh, you know, the usual holiday homecoming. How about you? Still running the family tree farm?"

Philip nodded, his expression a mix of pride and something more complex. "Sure am. It's a lot of work, but there's something special about being part of people's Christmas traditions."

Alexia thought back to the ornament she'd found earlier. "I was just thinking about you, actually. Remember that Christmas ornament you gave me in fourth grade?"

Philip's laugh echoed through the trees. "How could I forget? You were the first girl I gave a Christmas gift to—you know, that I wasn't related to."

"I found it stuffed in a drawer in my room just now."

Philip grinned.

As they walked and talked, Alexia found herself

studying Philip. He'd grown into his lanky frame, his shoulders broad beneath his warm jacket. But his eyes were the same—kind, with that spark of mischief she remembered so well.

"So, what's new in the big city?" Philip asked, his tone genuinely interested.

Alexia hesitated, unsure how to sum up years of life in a few sentences. "Oh, you know...work, friends, the usual. But being back here...it's making me realize how much I've missed this place."

Philip's gaze softened. "Well, we've missed you too, Lex. The town's not quite the same without its resident troublemaker."

Alexia laughed, feeling a warmth that had nothing to do with her winter coat. "Troublemaker? I seem to recall a certain someone who was always dragging me into his schemes."

As they continued to reminisce and catch up, Alexia felt the last of her nervousness melt away. There was something comforting about talking with Philip, like slipping on a favorite sweater she'd forgotten she owned.

About the Author

Award-winning author Kayla Lowe writes women's fiction that explores complex themes with sensitivity and depth. Kayla's books delve into the intricacies of relationships, self-discovery, and resilience. From cozy love stories interspersed with a bit of faith to heartwarming tales of friendship and suspenseful novels of empowerment and heartbreak, her books illustrate the struggles specific to women.

When she's not churning out her next novel, you can find her with her feet in the sand and a book in her hand or curled up on the couch with her dogs.

Visit her website at www.authorkaylalowe.com.

Also by Kayla Lowe

Series

Women of the Bible Fiction

Ruth

Esther

Rachel

Hannah

Deborah

Charms of the Chaste Court

A Courtship in Covent Garden

Whispers in Westminster

Romance in Regent's Park

Serenade on Strand Street

Treasure in Tower Bridge

Sweet Honey by the Sea

The Beekeeper's Secret (Book 1)

A Royal Honeycomb (Book 2)

Bees in Blossom (Book 3)

Honeyed Kisses (Book 4)

Blooming Forever (Book 5)

Strawberry Beach Series

Beachside Lessons (Book 1)

Beachside Lessons (Book 2)

Beachside Lessons (Book 3)

Panama City Beach Series

Sun-Kissed Secrets (Book 1)

Sun-Kissed Secrets (Book 2)

Sun-Kissed Secrets (Book 3)

The Tainted Love Saga

Of Love and Deception (Book 1)

Of Love and Family (Book 2)

Of Love and Violence (Book 3)

Of Love and Abuse(Book 4)

Of Love and Crime (Book 5)

Of Love and Addiction (Book 6)

Of Love and Redemption (Book 7)

Standalones

Maiden's Blush

Poetry

Phantom Poetry

Lost and Found

www.ingramcontent.com/pod-product-compliance
Lightning Source LLC
LaVergne TN
LVHW041230150826
845673LV00008B/2337

* 9 7 9 8 2 3 0 8 1 9 0 2 8 *